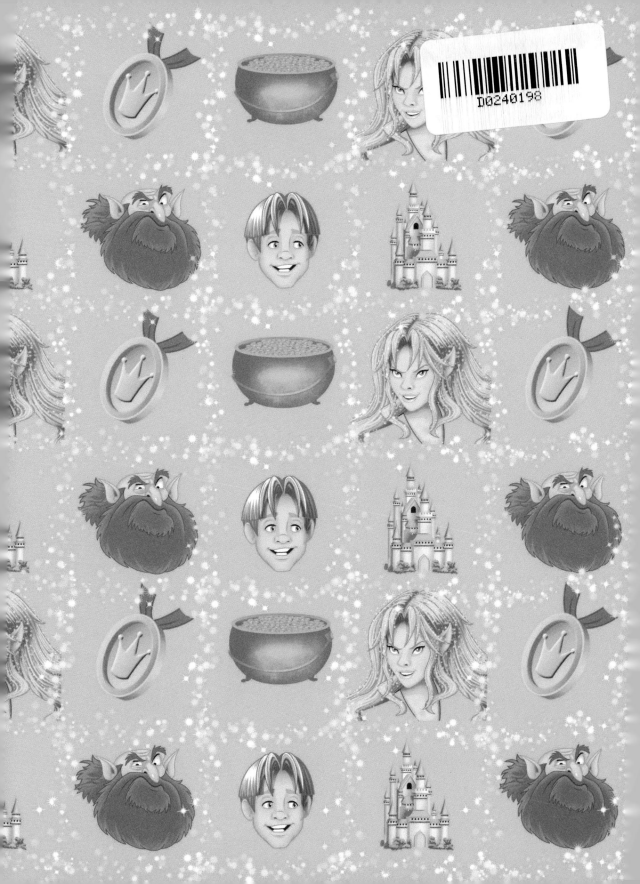

Princess Sabrina

and the
Pot of Gold

Written by Michael Pellico
Illustrated by Malane Newman

This book is dedicated to:
Sabrina Pellico
The inspiration for this story...
and many others.

And to my mother:
Helen Pellico
My hero and guiding light
throughout my life.

First Print Edition
ISBN 978-1-7339130-3-4
Printed in USA

Table of Contents

Chapter 1

A Visit to Ireland

Looking out the plane window, Avery, a tall, handsome, athletic boy just turning 15; his 13 year old sister, Renee, who loves to think of herself more worldly and wise for her age; and Elias, their quiet, 12 year old best friend get very excited when they spot the coast of Ireland. They are visiting their cousin Brian, and this is their first trip to another country!

They can hardly control their excitement. A boy who's about 13 is waiting for them at the baggage claim. He rushes up to them with a yell and a smiling face full of freckles. Brian has bright red hair that bobs when he talks.

After a happy and excited welcome, they drive through the beautiful green rolling hills of Ireland, past grazing sheep and the stone and wooden bridges crossing the many streams and creeks that run down from the hills. They roll past immense, dark, mysterious woods.

Finally, they approach the small village where their cousin lives. The thatched roofs, cobblestone streets, and old stone

bridge crossing the clear stream are enchanting for the children, who know only their home in Chicago.

For the next few days, the children explore the village and the ancient woods surrounding it. However, the most exciting thing is the ruined castle overlooking the village from a high hill. Exploring the ruins makes the children imagine life in Ireland a long time ago in the age of knights, dragons, princes, and princesses.

Chapter 1: A Visit to Ireland

One day, Brian's parents have to fly to London for a business meeting, so they leave the children with Ariel, the babysitter, until they return.

A couple days later, Avery is sitting on the old stone bridge, gazing at the bubbling stream and the small, colorful fish darting among the rocks. He senses a stillness in the air. It is as if the whole forest is waiting in anticipation of a big event. Avery wonders how the animals know a storm is coming.

He can see dark, billowing clouds hovering on the horizon, and he is aware the stillness is a prelude to strong winds that will push the storm closer. He can see bolts of lightning in the distance, which are followed by peals of thunder that sound closer and closer. He hurries home to make sure everyone is safely inside. Waiting for the storm to come, the children play games, make popcorn, and talk about the differences between Ireland and America.

When it gets dark, the storm finally hits with howling winds shaking the house and everyone inside. The children huddle around the stone fireplace, somehow feeling safer— especially when lightning strikes nearby, and the lights in the house flicker and go dead for a few moments. The sky lights up every few seconds with powerful bolts of lightning that fell huge trees and take out the power to the whole village.

Chapter 2

The Rainbow's End

· ·

Finally, morning comes. Avery is groggy from staying up all night with his sister Renee, Elias and Brian, listening to the adventures and scary stories Ariel told. The airport is closed because of the violent storm, and Brian's parents are unable to come home.

Ariel has agreed to watch the children until they arrive the next day. She keeps them entertained with games and more stories. Avery is a little upset that his aunt and uncle hired a babysitter. He is sure he's old enough to keep everyone safe and wishes they would understand he is a young man!

Avery fumbles his way out of bed. Before he can do much more than toss on some old clothes, Renee rushes in, tugging him downstairs to join Elias and Brian in the garden and stare at what must be the largest, most vibrant rainbow that ever lit up an after-rain sky.

The rainbow seems so solid a car could drive on it. The colors are the brightest the children have ever seen in a rainbow, and it seems closer to the ground than the ones in Chicago ever did. Avery strangely feels that somehow, this rainbow will never fade. The sight takes his breath away. The incredible beauty of the rainbow makes all thoughts of staying home disappear. Only the desire to chase after the light of the rainbow and find its end remains in the children's minds.

They all know the story about leprechauns and the pot of gold that is supposed to be at the end of the rainbow. Many times in the past, they tried to follow a rainbow to its end, but each time, the rainbow faded away before they could reach it. This time, somehow it feels different!

Brian says, "I've never seen anything like this before." He tells the children he knows these woods and begs them to follow him. What an adventure we can share with our friends back home, they think.

They hesitate for a second and then race out the door, rushing through the old-growth forest on the outskirts of the village. Every time they grow tired from the endless crawl through the tangled trees and dew-covered ferns, the sight of the rainbow breaking through the leaves closer and closer to their reach brings new life to their fatigued limbs. Sometimes, even the path is hard to follow because the high storm winds left behind branches.

Chapter 2: The Rainbow's End

Finally, after what seems like an eternity, the children stumble into a clearing at the center of the woods. There, the rainbow comes to an end—a seemingly solid bridge of intense, bright colors. The dark-green moss, multicolored spring flowers, and wheat-gold grass shimmer in its light.

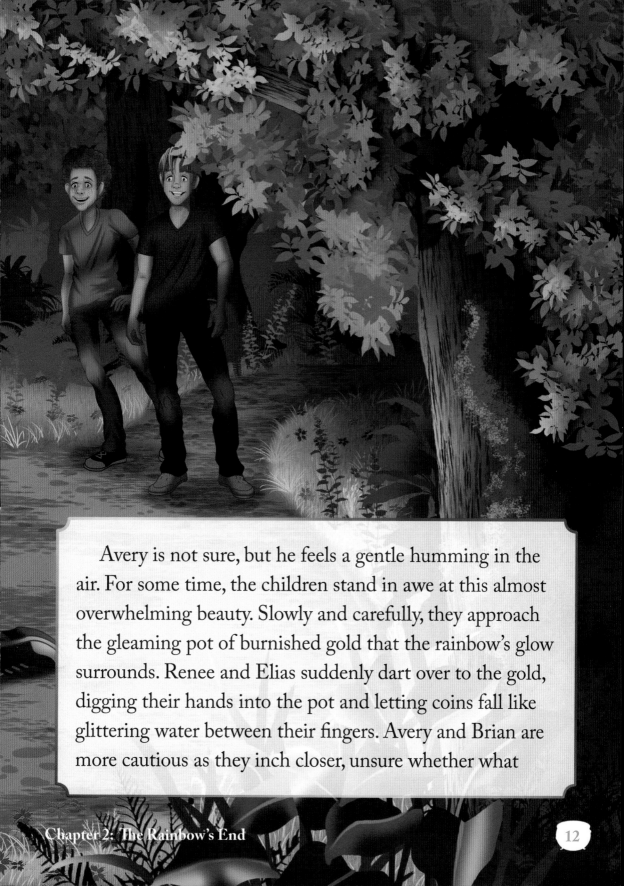

Avery is not sure, but he feels a gentle humming in the air. For some time, the children stand in awe at this almost overwhelming beauty. Slowly and carefully, they approach the gleaming pot of burnished gold that the rainbow's glow surrounds. Renee and Elias suddenly dart over to the gold, digging their hands into the pot and letting coins fall like glittering water between their fingers. Avery and Brian are more cautious as they inch closer, unsure whether what they are seeing is even real. Reaching out and touching the coins very much proves their existence. Each coin features an intricate carving of a beautiful girl with delicate features, commanding eyes, and wild hair tied in knots that move the image as if it were alive. Avery is struck by the urge to find this girl—an urge stronger than anything he's felt before. The feeling catches him off guard, shaking him from his stupor and bringing him back to reality.

Avery gathers the other children, and they decide to take the gold back home to split among themselves. They talk eagerly about what they will do with all the money. They realize it would free them from the money struggles their parents try to hide from them. But the second they move the pot from its position, a sound reverberates through the clearing like a massive door slamming shut. The brilliant rainbow fades to nothing, leaving a faint trace that can be seen only at certain angles when the light hits just right.

The children are spooked both by the heavy noise and the sudden sounds coming from the forest around them like scampering feet through the underbrush just out of sight. The shadows of the trees and ferns seem darker and threatening without the rainbow to brighten the surroundings, but Avery urges them on. Because the pot is heavy, they make a rough sled out of Avery's jacket and drag the gold home.

That night, exhausted from the trek back with the heavy pot of gold, the children stay awake talking excitedly. They stare at the gold in hushed silence, almost believing it might disappear at any moment.

Unbeknownst to them, a shadow lurks outside their window with a dangerous smile and glittering teeth in the moonlight; it dashes through the night and then vanishes. The children stuff handfuls of gold into their pockets, unable to resist the solid coins, which are proof that magic must exist in the world—and that what they'd experienced wasn't a dream. The excitement of finding the treasure teems beneath their skin, and their urge to tell their parents is almost impossible to ignore. But the children are determined to keep such an incredible secret to themselves.

Finally, they fall asleep with the pot of gold hidden in the back of Avery's closet. It isn't long before the shadow who stalked them throughout the day acts. Without a sound or waking them up, he whisks the sleeping children away from their beds and carries them far from their world.

Chapter 3

Kingdom's Hidden Truth

hen Avery next awakens, he finds himself on soft wild-silk blankets in a sunlit room with beautiful stone walls and pleated purple curtains. Renee, Elias, and Brian sleep in the beds beside his. Avery quickly walks over to make sure they're okay.

The doors open, and a person enters, regal and proudly dressed in green and gold. The large fur cape around his shoulders drapes almost to the floor. Although he looks human, his ears are short and pointed. He stands just over five feet tall, and he is strong with well-muscled arms and legs. His hair is a strange orange-brown color, and a bushy, unkempt beard covers the lower part of his face. To Avery, it seems the worn-looking clothes have seen better days. Avery is wary, keeping the others behind him until Renee and the others wriggle out of bed to face this strange being.

"I am King Bran, the king of the leprechauns," the man announces as he smiles and bows before them. He tells them they are in the Fae Kingdom, and they are guests in his castle. Still smiling, King Bran earnestly says that all he wants is his gold back for the good of the kingdom.

The children listen in amazement. "Why should we return it when we found it?" Elias pipes up. "And why was the gold under the rainbow in the first place?"

A shadow seems to pass over the King's face, but he quickly hides it with a forced smile saying, "We need the gold to maintain the link between the Fae Kingdom and the Human Realm, held together by the rainbow and the Royal Clan Line of the Leprechauns."

Without the gold, the king explains, the leprechaun kingdom will decay, drained of its magic. The gold is the only way to strengthen the rainbow and make it into a magical path between worlds. The king explains that the human world contains minerals the leprechaun world lacks, which it needs for good health.

Before the children can decide, the King holds up his hand and tells them to think it over while they enjoy their stay, leaving them with a pleasant guard to tour the castle with them while he deals with other matters. The reality of their stay in a magical realm hits them, and they spend the rest of the day exploring the castle and its grounds, swept away by the beauty around them. The castle is majestic with

Chapter 3: Kingdom's Hidden Truth

arches, green tile floors, flowers and plants in every corner, and beautifully carved wooden benches and other furniture.

That night, after the guard leads them back to their rooms, the children discuss the gold and decide they should give it back. After all, it seems more important to keep the realms connected than retain the gold for their own needs. In the middle of the night, a new shadow slips into their room. It's another leprechaun, appearing to be about the same age as Renee and Brian. The young leprechaun reveals he is Prince Riordan, the younger brother of the real ruler of the kingdom, Princess Sabrina.

Avery remembers the beautiful girl on the coins as he and the others hear that King Bran betrayed his brother—the former king—by poisoning him, and then captured Princess Sabrina. King Bran told the kingdom the princess had killed her father and ran away, and they were searching for her. Prince Riordan explains that he went into hiding before the king could capture him too, and accuse him of being a traitor for aiding in his father's death.

But Princess Sabrina, the actual ruler, is a prisoner deep in the castle dungeons where not even her allies can help her. Her brother tells the shocked children that outside the palace, the rest of the realm is decaying without its rightful heiress to hold the magic together, although few suspect the king because he is a part of the Royal Clan Line and bears the medallion of the clan's right to rule—stolen from Sabrina when she was captured. Because the prince has also vanished, the leprechaun people had no choice but to accept Bran as their ruler. However, because the medallion is not with the real ruler and the pot of gold is not in its place at the end of the rainbow, the king can't stop the decay. Prince Riordan, with anger in his voice, tells the children the false king has led the people astray and no longer protects the forest and the people and creatures who dwell there. A true leprechaun king would never wear the fur of an animal!

Riordan's face lights up with hope when he tells the children they may be able to help save his sister because his evil uncle, King Bran, won't suspect they know the truth. He comes up with a plan and tells the children the details. Avery and the others listen with interest, and they agree to help.

"I know the way to the dungeons," Riordan says. "If we stay together, we can sneak past the guards." The prince explains about the magical wards that warn the guards about intruders—but he says they cannot recognize humans, and they will not recognize him because he is a royal. Some of the wards are magical creatures, and others are both visible

Chapter 3: Kingdom's Hidden Truth

and invisible spells. He says the guards will not stop the children if they say they are exploring the castle with the king's permission. "I will wear a disguise," Riordan says, "so the guards will think I am human."

That night, the children steal away past the guards and make their way to the princess, passing by the wards with ease before arriving at her dimly lit cell. Quickly unlocking the heavy door, they step inside. When the princess sees her brother, she rushes up to him.

"I missed you so much," she says, hugging him gleefully. She asks about the children, and Riordan explains what happened and says they are there to help her regain her kingdom.

Although Princess Sabrina is about the same age as Avery, he is blown away by her beauty and regal presence when she speaks to their group. Even though she's been locked up for so long, the fierceness in her eyes and sharpness of her mind enchant him more than her flawless etching he saw on the coins did. Sabrina has the most amazing green eyes that seem to sparkle in the candlelight, and her hair is a soft golden green. Although her clothes are ragged and dirty, Avery can see that her body is lithe, and she moves with the smoothness of a warrior princess.

Chapter 4

Escaping the Castle

They waste no time getting Princess Sabrina away from the castle, slowing only to avoid the guards and magical wards guarding the castle's long corridors. They are stopped several times, but the children hide the prince and princess, confusing the guards. They tell the guards they are human, and the king has given them the right to explore the castle.

Suddenly, near the castle walls, Princess Sabrina sets off a magical alarm! Guards rush toward them to block their escape. Quickly, Prince Riordan pulls out his sword and slashes ropes holding barrels of oil which tumble down and break open, spilling oil over the guards. Avery grabs a torch and throws it on the spreading oil, which immediately bursts into flames. Panicking, the guards run away before the fire can reach them.

Running across the drawbridge and into the dark woods, the party comes across loyal followers of the prince who have been waiting on the outskirts. Quietly but swiftly, the group makes its way to the resistance base, where they meet the rebels Riordan has been gathering to rescue Sabrina. They welcome her to the camp with clapping, smiling faces, and celebratory cheer. That night, there are songs and dancing for the return of the princess and renewed hope that the kingdom would soon have its rightful ruler back so it could start to heal.

Avery and the children are fascinated by the many creatures they meet, and they are excited to be on such an adventure. Avery can see—away from the singing and dancing—Princess Sabrina holding counsel with Prince Riordan and several other leprechauns.

Now that they have time to look around, Avery and the others notice the signs of decay that have been eating away at the land. When Sabrina questions the gathering about the extent of the Fae Kingdom's decay, people come forward with disheartening tales about what drove them from their homes. Sabrina turns to the children, wiping the fear from her face. "Please, help us take back our kingdom," she asks.

The prince tells the children "adults cannot find the pot of gold because only children can see the magic around them. The rainbow will only let the pure of heart find the pot of gold and chose you because it knew you would help us fight our evil uncle and make the land of the leprechauns happy and free again."

Avery looks at his sister, Elias and Brian and, seeing the determination in their eyes, replies, "Of course we will help, but we're only human. We have no magical powers or combat training." This prompts smiles and laughter from the leprechauns.

"Humans have great power over creatures in this land— not in a magical capacity, but in their ability to wield tools made from cold iron, silver, and nickel," says Sabrina. The children are tasked with retrieving great weapons the leprechauns took from humans they'd battled long ago when their realms were more closely connected. Avery and the others join Riordan and Sabrina to help them on their journey, leaving the camp behind to rally the troops in preparation for war.

Chapter 5

The Quest for Magic Weapons

They venture deeply into the realm's most ancient corners, their speed hastened by the magical insect-like creatures, that look like large dragonflies, the leprechauns use for travel.

The first weapon location is over the foggy Black Moors, precarious to traverse with their hidden holes and unstable ground. The party makes its way along, picking out a path and avoiding the watery depths. They have a brief scare when Brian slips and falls into a gap, only to be saved by Elias's quick grab at his grasping hands before he slips fully under the surface. They find a sacred fairy mound in the center of the moor and retrieve a silver dagger which Elias pulls out of its holder and claims. When he removes the dagger, the moor vanishes as if it were an illusion, replaced by a serene meadow.

The next location is over Mag Mell, a perpetually stormy lake inhabited by a great and terrible serpent that defends it from trespassers. The group boards swift brown wooden boats tied to a rickety dock. Each boat holds only three people. Avery ends up with Renee and Sabrina—much to his joy and panic—while Riordan goes with Brian and Elias. They make their way over the rough waters almost to the island at the center of the lake when the serpent, a water dragon hiding in the depths, suddenly rises to the surface and nearly overturns them, sinking into the water like a dark knife to make another attempt.

"Only music can calm the serpent," Riordan explains. He curses their lack of any way to pacify it. Riordan has a terrible singing voice, and he's never gotten the hang of it despite all the practice Fae children receive. The serpent

Chapter 5: The Quest for Magic Weapons

32

attacks the other boat, capsizing it and leaving Avery, Sabrina, and Renee floundering in the waves.

Brian—hesitant at first because he's shy about his abilities—sings a lullaby, trying to keep his voice steady as fear for his friends makes him waver. At first, the serpent rages harder, almost hitting Avery and Sabrina as they desperately try to keep themselves and Renee above water. Hearing encouragement from Elias and Riordan, Brian makes himself sing louder, and his voice penetrates the storm, soothing the thrashing serpent enough to let the others get back into their boat.

They make their way to the island, finding the fairy mound at its center and revealing the next artifact—a gilded harp—with strings capable of sending to sleep anyone who wants to harm the player. Brian steps forward to claim it, smiling in awe at the instrument. When they leave the mound, a path opens from the island to the shore, and the storm clears, letting them cross back safely.

When they reach land, a group of mermaids suddenly hails them from the waters, revealing that the raging serpent had kept them trapped in its depths. The mermaids look alike with long, seaweed-like hair and sparkling, silvery tails. They thank Sabrina and the others for calming the creature, pledging their services to her cause and promising to help in any way they can. The mermaids are fascinated by the sight of the humans and crowd around them asking questions and touching them shyly.

Sabrina smiles. "Thanks for your help, but I have to remind everyone that it was Brian who saved the day," she says. Brian smiles proudly when the princess gazes at him.

Chapter 6

The First Battle

lowly they strike out from the lake. The ordeal has tired them, but they push themselves on, having to travel across a vast plain to reach their next objective.

Suddenly, they are surrounded by the king's troops, who have been searching for the escaped princess and have finally caught up with her. Thankfully, it is only a scouting party of four leprechauns and four creatures loyal to the king!

This is the children's first battle, and Brian and Avery hesitate, unsure of how to help. Elias immediately joins Renee, Princess Sabrina, and Riordan to rush the enemies. Seeing Renee running headlong into danger without a weapon spurs Brian and Avery into motion to defend the others. Sabrina and Riordan are expert fighters, but the scouts are well armed.

After a difficult fight, Prince Riordan, Princess Sabrina, and the group manage to prevail, although not before one of the scouts flees to report their location to the king. Knowing they need to hurry, they tend to the few minor wounds they received and continue on.

Throughout the rest of the journey, the king's men harass their group, but luck and their growing skill gained from each battle enable to stay one step ahead of the enemies and continue moving forward. Although Renee and Avery still don't have their weapons, they take some of the enemy's swords and use them in the meantime.

Finally, Castle Danu looms on the horizon with moss-covered stone towers reaching toward the sky like beacons. Numerous enemies block their way, so the group stops. They know they cannot fight through so many. Seeing no other way to get inside, Riordan comes up with a desperate plan he shares with Sabrina. "You have to turn me over to our enemies," Riordan tells her.

"What?" Sabrina says. "Are you crazy?"

"Turn me over as a distraction to allow the others to slip into the castle unseen," Riordan insists.

Despite attempts by the others to change his mind, no other ideas are forthcoming, and Riordan begins to head toward the enemy. However, another leprechaun dressed in the uniform of the king's army suddenly comes up behind them.

"Don't worry. I'm on your side," says the soldier, Seamus.

"I just want to help. If one of you borrows my uniform, you can get into the castle."

Renee immediately offers to go, despite Avery's protests. But she convinces them that she must because the next magical weapon is hers. "I can feel it calling out to me," she says. They reluctantly let her go and watch as Seamus helps her into his uniform and gives her tips on how to blend into the ranks.

Renee stalks forward, her hair hiding her ears and the helmet low on her forehead to cover as much of her face as possible. Her heart thundering in her chest, she makes her way through the leprechaun army, strolling as casually as she can toward the castle.

Just as she is about to make it inside, a commanding leprechaun stops her and demands to know why she is trying to get in. Not bothering to offer an excuse, Renee attacks and pushes past him.

She rushes the last few steps into the castle and toward the stairs while the enemy pursues her. She can feel she is close to the weapon. The guards run past Renee as she hides in a tiny alcove.

When the coast is clear, she runs down the long corridor. Breaking into the last room at the top, Renee moves toward an apparently empty spot on the stone wall, senses where

her magical weapon is.

She reaches up and grabs at an invisible fabric, wrapping herself in it just as the door is flung open and a leprechaun enters. He searches for Renee but is unable to see her while she is wrapped in her new invisible cloak.

She quietly slips away and runs down the stairs while the leprechauns curse at the empty room. Angered at her escape, the commander of the guards tells his men to search every corner because he smells a human! When she makes it outside the castle, the king's army is in an uproar. They try to find the intruder in their midst, and the growing enemy outside the castle is starting to make them panic.

Through the chaos, Renee slips past the leprechauns and heads outside toward the growing group. Renee marches up and stands in front of them, unseen. Everyone is startled when she whips off the cloak and grins at their shocked faces, giving a thumbs-up to confirm her success. The group lets out a collective sigh of relief as Princess Sabrina thanks Seamus for his assistance and congratulates Renee on her daring escape. Seamus blushes and shrugs bashfully at the gratitude from his princess.

Chapter 7

Journey Back to the Kingdom

As they travel back to the base, Sabrina and Riordan share a quiet discussion before telling the children that the last weapon, the Great Sword, is in the hands of the king—and they're not sure how to get it back.

Crossing the kingdom, they find the land has weakened even more as the decay spread to even more towns. They enter the base and prepare for their next battle. After speaking with some of the elder leprechauns who have worked in the castle, the group learns of a secret entry to the Throne Room, where the sword is likely to be, although they will still have to get into the castle first.

They leave the base once more, heading back to the dangers of the castle. The journey back to the castle is more treacherous than before. Armed garrisons of leprechauns pass by while the group hides just out of sight, tucked behind Renee's cloak as much as possible. They endure the rest of the journey the same way, each moment filled with tense silence and close scares. They are forced to overcome a few scouts that nearly find them.

The group just makes it to the castle, finding the hidden tunnel beneath the wall that lets them slip inside. Making their way along aided by magical lighting, they head toward the Throne Room. A door shimmers into existence at the end, opening at Princess Sabrina's touch. A dark room greets them, and they hesitantly step inside.

There, on a pedestal, is a gleaming sword made of cold iron and encased in runes to protect Fae from its deadly touch. The sword was won after victory over a great human king. Riordan and Sabrina stare at it with a mixture of awe and apprehension, knowing it is one of the deadliest weapons against leprechauns. Avery stares at the blade, feeling the pull of its magic but unsure whether he is capable of handling something so destructive. Knowing they don't have time for him to dwell on that fear, Avery goes to claim the sword, but just as he reaches for it, the doors of the Throne Room open, and the king strides in, stopping in outrage at the sight of the princess.

The king rushes them, drawing his sword. Riordan jumps forward and defends them while Avery reaches past the runes and takes the sword, racing to join Riordan. However, the shouts draw the guards' attention, and enemies quickly flood the Throne Room, moving to the king's defense.

Seeing that they are outnumbered, the group flees to the tunnel—but not before Riordan is captured. Much as she wants to return to her brother, Sabrina knows that would only get the rest of them captured, too. Fighting back tears, she urges them onward, despite their protests.

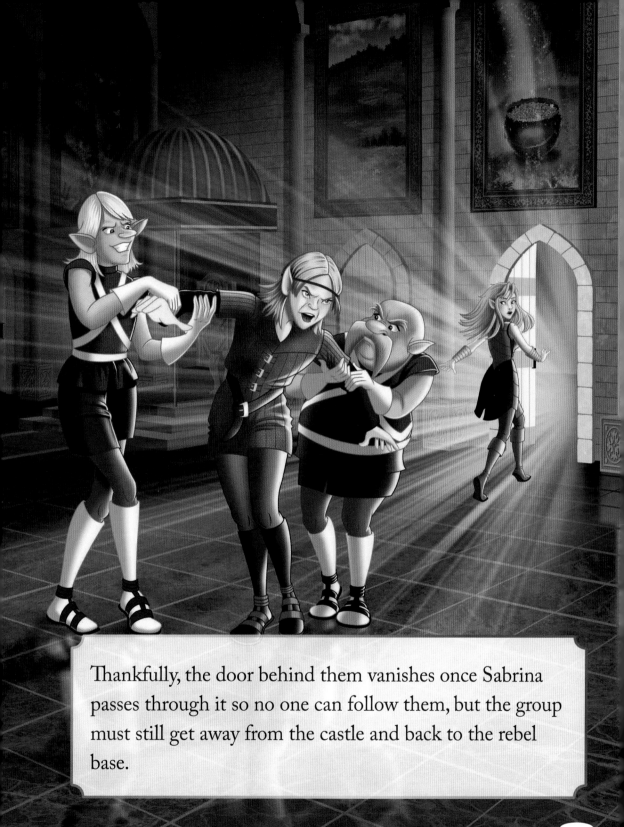

Thankfully, the door behind them vanishes once Sabrina passes through it so no one can follow them, but the group must still get away from the castle and back to the rebel base.

Chapter 8

A Sullen Party

The return trip is filled with bitter silence. Sabrina is happy they were able to retrieve the weapon, but she dreads having to break the news of Riordan's capture to the camp, knowing how morale will drop. She fights with her feelings of guilt the whole way back. The others are also unable to get past losing Riordan, wondering whether they should have gone back for him.

It's a sullen party, despite Elias's attempts to lighten the mood despite his own bad feelings and Brian's attempts at consoling. Avery tells Sabrina it's not her fault, assuring her they'll get Riordan back, comforting her, and eventually getting a small smile for his efforts.

Avery musters his courage and takes Sabrina's hand in his, gripping it to give her a way to steady herself, even though she is trying to be strong on her own. Sabrina takes a shuddering breath and grips his hand back, taking strength from his presence. She leads them back to camp, and they arrive to find that the situation is dire at the outskirts of the kingdom. Thousands of magical creatures have fled to the camp's relative safety.

The rest of the day is spent mobilizing the troops. Avery helps Sabrina until she refers to him as her general. Avery is delighted and proud of the confidence the princess has in him, and his heart beats faster when he is near her. Unknown to Avery, Sabrina secretly steals a glance whenever he's not looking, and her little heart beats faster, too.

That night, they sleep restlessly, unable to calm themselves enough to drift off. The reality of having to fight in an actual war weighs on the children's minds. As dangerous as the journey has been so far, it hadn't really hit them until Riordan was captured that they might be fighting for their lives. Even the previous battles had seemed like more of a game or adventure than a real fight, despite the very real danger they'd experienced.

But dawn comes, and they arm themselves for war. Princess Sabrina is dressed in a long-sleeved emerald-green leather tunic and darker green leather pants with a black belt and a short, narrow sword. Her subjects bow their heads. She delivers a fierce speech, drawing forth a roar from the crowd, and she puts on the Queen's Crown—an artifact Riordan had managed to take from the castle when he fled, knowing Princess Sabrina would need it as a symbol of her power and right to rule in place of the false king. Sabrina thinks about her father, remembering how he'd let her play with his crown as he taught her all the duties and responsibilities she would need to learn to protect her kingdom.

They set out. Sabrina and their group lead the troops, traveling awhile before coming to one of the enemy camps. It is one of the many strategically located around the outskirts of the kingdom as a first line of defense, and defeating them is easy. A scout is able to send a warning message to the king of their location, and they realize they will have to face the final battle.

Chapter 9

The Final Battle

They make their way to the Great Plains surrounding the kingdom and gaze across them to the king's amassed troops. Sabrina tries to get the enemy troops to join her, but they are too convinced of her guilt to be swayed. The king calls for the traitor's crown, and the battle begins.

Avery is split from the group immediately, and the battle quickly becomes chaotic. He desperately fights to find his sister and is only just able to make out Brian and Elias in another part of the frenzy. They each use their respective weapons. Brian's harp drops those enemies nearest him like flies, while the ones who hear it on the vicinity become drowsy, and their opponents easily defeat them. Elias protects Brian with his silver dagger, stopping any who attempt to cut his friend down and working as an extension of Brian's reach.

Avery spots Sabrina—a whirling dervish on the battlefield—and goes to join her, hoping she's seen Renee. Pitting his hard-won skills against seasoned soldiers strains Avery to his limits, and he fights through the crush of bodies.

He makes it to Sabrina's side, receiving a fierce grin when she sees him. Avery smiles back at her and, wielding his powerful enchanted sword, battles by her side as they move closer to the king. He's able to ask Sabrina whether she's seen Renee but only receives a sharp shake of her head in the negative. Avery can only hope his sister is safe beneath her invisibility cloak. He forces himself to move past his worries for her.

They work together in a brilliant show of teamwork, defending each other's blind spots and dropping their opponents with swinging blows of their weapons. Avery begins to relish the adrenalin rush and starts overcoming his fear of battle, feeling more confident and alive than he's ever felt before. He gets an insane impulse to kiss Sabrina in the middle of the fighting but settles for blocking a sword aimed at her head and knocking the attacker back instead. When he spots Sabrina looking at him, he feels renewed strength.

They just reach the bottom of the hill the king stands atop when he spots them. A wicked grin spreads across the king's face before he motions to the soldiers beside him, and Avery and Sabrina notice the covered cage that had been hidden by an illusion the whole time. There, in the cage, is Riordan, chained and bedraggled. Sabrina gasps in a combination of anger and relief that her brother is alive, glaring at her evil Uncle Bran before steadily battling up the hill and slashing through combatants. Avery follows her, overcoming anyone attacking her from behind.

The king sneers at them as they get closer, calling to his men to notch their arrows. Sabrina stops, levels her long, narrow sword at her uncle, and shouts above the battlefield noise that he should release her brother, surrender, step down from the throne, and return the medallion to its rightful place. The king scowls and walks toward her a few

steps, crossing his arms and directing her attention back to her brother when he orders the archers to aim at Riordan instead.

Wielding a large powerful ax, King Bran challenges Sabrina to one-on-one combat, accusing her of treason against the throne and saying a trial is too good for her, but because she was previously heiress to the crown, he will allow it. Sabrina narrows her eyes, but she agrees to the king's proposal for fear he will order the soldiers to draw back their bows and shoot her brother.

Avery stands back, feeling frustration rising as he realizes he won't be able to step into the fight—though he promises himself he will if it looks like the king is about to strike a killing blow, regardless of the leprechaun customs he would be breaking. Steadied, Avery settles back, wary and ready to step in if he needs to.

Sabrina smiles back at him before turning to meet her uncle. With an angry, triumphant yell, King Bran rushes forward and swings his heavy ax as if it were as light as a feather. Sabrina's speed and the years of her father's training enable her to dodge all the king's blows. Moving swiftly and constantly, Sabrina darts under the ax and keeps slashing away at the king. She backs away, stumbles on a rock, and falls. The king, sensing victory, yells and swings a deadly blow at Sabrina—but she quickly rolls aside, and the ax crashes into a rock where her head has just been.

The battlefield around them has slowed to a stop as the two armies realize the real fight for the kingdom is happening on the hilltop. It's almost impossible for Avery to take his eyes off the battle, but he remembers Riordan and sees that he's still trapped in the cage.

Edging carefully around the hilltop and keeping his eyes on the enemy soldiers, who are focused on the fight, Avery makes his way to the cage. With a strong swing of his sword, he breaks the lock and helps the prince out while the archers are distracted by the clash. They turn to join the battle when an enormous roar comes from the onlookers. Avery jerks his attention back toward the fight, freezing at what he sees.

Sabrina moves toward the backward-walking king, who is unable to keep swinging his heavy ax so quickly. Suddenly, the ax drops from his hand, and he stumbles to the ground, breathing heavily. Sabrina, not trusting him, leaps at him with her long narrow sword aimed at his throat. Gasping and covered with battle wounds, she stands victorious and orders her uncle to surrender and hand over the medallion. Her voice rings out over the battlefield, amplified by magic to reach everyone's ears, "the battle is

Chapter 9: The Final Battle

over, lay down your weapons, now we must join together to rebuild our wonderful world"

The king bows his head in apparent defeat; the moment pauses in time like a held breath as everyone waits for his surrender. The king raises his head to look at Sabrina. An ugly expression of rage crosses his face before he abruptly turns and throws one of his knives at her.

Avery glances toward Sabrina, seeing her expression of surprise and anger. Suddenly, Sabrina is knocked off her feet, and the dagger flashes by and hits a tree behind her.

Renee appears, and they realize she had been standing next to Sabrina, hidden beneath her invisibility cloak. It is she who has knocked the princess out of the dagger's path. Avery hugs her tightly, relieved that she is safe. Before he can ask Renee anything, their attention is drawn back to Sabrina and the king—and the sudden uproar coming from both their armies.

Sabrina is standing while her uncle is detained and brought to his knees before her by his own soldiers. Avery and Renee walk over to Sabrina to see what's happening. Sabrina smiles when she sees them, bringing Avery into a fierce hug that hurts his wounds, but he can't bring himself to mind. She gives one to Renee too and thanking her for her bravery and quick thinking.

"Why did the king's men turn on him?" Avery asks.

"Because he broke the laws of combat and attacked someone outside the fight after he'd been defeated," Sabrina says.

Walking up to her glaring uncle Sabrina again demands the medallion. The king grins sadistically.

"You can have your medallion," he says, "but your brother will die in that cage because only I know the whereabouts of the magic key needed to unlock it." Everyone laughs as Riordan steps forward and tells his uncle that Avery has broken the lock with his enchanted sword. Renee also laughs as she steps forward and holds out the ornate key.

King Bran gasps in outrage. Renee had slipped the key away from him earlier in the fight and waited until she could get Riordan out unnoticed.

Sabrina smiles in triumph when the king realizes he's out of moves, bowing his head and letting Sabrina remove the medallion. Sabrina stands again and sets the necklace around her neck where it belongs and, as it settles, magic bursts forth from the gold at its center, rushing out over the land and off into the distance, reversing the decay that has plagued the realm. The soldiers around the field nearly fall to their knees as the decay many hadn't even realized was weakening them disappears, and they felt better than they have in a long time.

A cheer rises up from the armies, and Elias and Brian rush out of the crowd to join the group on the hill—battered and wounded, but sharing in the joy around them, laughter splitting their faces into wide grins. After making sure everyone in their group is all right, Sabrina separates from them and turns to address the crowd and her uncle.

"For too long, our beloved kingdom and all that dwelled within have suffered from the false king. Now our good magic will go strong again. My father was a king who loved this land and all of his subjects. And he taught me how to be a queen who would be just and humble. Please help me to rebuild our kingdom and together we will be greater than ever before!"

After she gives the speech, she decrees that her uncle will remain locked up for his crimes.

Taking the key from Renee, Sabrina has the soldiers remove her uncle's weapons and lock him inside the cage with a new lock strengthened by a magic spell.

Riordan walks up to his sister, and they watch as Bran is carried away in the cage that once imprisoned the prince. Riordan bows to his sister saying, "You'll make a great queen."

Chapter 10

Journey's End

· ·

Everyone returns to the palace while the wounded and dead are tended to, and Avery realizes their journey has come to an end. Avery, Renee, Elias, and Brian stand in the throne room before Sabrina and Riordan to accept gifts for their help.

Queen Sabrina sits on the stone throne dressed in a beautiful green gown with gold trim. Avery is transfixed by her regal bearing and beauty and realizes that he is in the presence of a truly special queen.

"Each of you has earned a wish," Sabrina tells the children. "You can wish for anything you can dream of, but you must think wisely about what it is you want."

Avery listens as the others talked excitedly about what they will wish for. He gazes at Sabrina, already knowing his decision. Renee steps up first and says she wants to keep her cloak when she returns to the real world. Elias follows and asks for long, healthy, happy lives for himself and the people he loves. Brian hesitates and asks if Sabrina could heal his mother from her painful back condition. She nods kindly and waits for Avery to make his wish. After a while, Avery takes a shuddering breath, walks up to Sabrina, and smiles.

"All I want to wish for is to be able to see you again," Avery says.

Sabrina blushes and grins back at him. She rises from the throne and dances down a few steps to stand in front of Avery. Sabrina kneels to kiss him softly, and a glow envelops them as she grants their wishes.

Queen Sabrina chants as she backs away from Avery and the children, pointing at an open area as she goes. Suddenly, a rainbow appears. Sabrina turns to the children.

"Please, quickly go into the rainbow," she says. "It will take you home. Without a storm, I cannot keep it open long!"

Looking back, the children say goodbye and step into the rainbow, quickly disappearing. Avery, the last to step in, turns and bows as he walks back into the rainbow.

After they return to their own world, Avery still cannot shake Princess Sabrina from his mind. He often remembers, both fondly and wistfully, the faint kiss that still lingers on his lips and the knowledge that the gold has been returned to its pot under the rainbow. He smiles, knowing the two worlds are once again connected.

One night, many moons later, Avery is awakened from a

Chapter 10: Journey's End

deep sleep. A strange glow is outside his bedroom window. Staring out the window, he sees an amazing sight. There, in the light of a full moon, is a rainbow! Avery dresses quickly and hurries outside. The rainbow is different from any he has ever seen. It is a moonbow with colors that are pale yet stunning against the starry night sky.

Staring at that incredible magical sight, Avery is frozen when, suddenly, Queen Sabrina appears, dressed in the same outfit she wore in the battle, and as beautiful and graceful as he remembers her. She steps from the moonbow and walks toward him with a smile he will never forget...

The End

About the Author

Michael Pellico is a medical researcher, writer, and film producer. One of eleven children whose parents both worked long hours. It was his responsibility to help raise his siblings. Growing up "poor", he entertained them with stories, and later telling stories to their children. This book and all his stories are dedicated to Sabrina, his niece, who insists that he tell her a story each time they are together. We hope that you love them as much as Sabrina does!

About the Illustrator

Malane Newman is a professional freelance illustrator and cartoonist. Born and raised in San Diego, she grew up with a passion for cartoon illustration. She is self-taught and began as a traditional cartoonist and evolved to illustrating on computer many years ago. She is a master at creating eye candy with color and illustrates in many different cartooning styles. She has worked on famous properties like Barbie and Swan Princess. Her work has appeared on food and product packaging, board games, children's books, greeting cards, and other consumer products. We hope you love her art as much as she enjoyed creating it!